JON SCIESZKA'S TRUCKTOWN UH-OH, MAX

WRITTEN BY JON SCIESZKA

CHARACTERS AND ENVIRONMENTS DEVELOPED BY THE

DESIGN garage

DAVID SHANNON   LOREN LONG   DAVID GORDON

ILLUSTRATION CREW:

Executive producer: TOT INDUSTRIES in association with Animagic S.L.

Creative supervisor: Sergio Pablos ○ Drawings by: Juan Pablo Navas ○ Color by: Isabel Nadal

Color assistant: Gabriela Lazbal ○ Art director: Karin Paprocki

READY-TO-READ

SIMON SPOTLIGHT
NEW YORK   LONDON   TORONTO   SYDNEY

ABDO
Spotlight

ABDOPUBLISHING.COM

Reinforced library bound edition published in 2016 by Spotlight, a division of ABDO
PO Box 398166, Minneapolis, Minnesota 55439. Spotlight produces high-quality reinforced
library bound editions for schools and libraries. Published by agreement with Simon Spotlight.

Printed in the United States of America, North Mankato, Minnesota.
042015   092015

SIMON SPOTLIGHT

An imprint of Simon & Schuster Children's Publishing Division
1230 Avenue of the Americas, New York, NY 10020
First Simon Spotlight paperback edition January 2009
Copyright © 2009 by JRS Worldwide, LLC. TRUCKTOWN AND JON SCIESZKA'S
TRUCKTOWN and design are trademarks of JRS Worldwide, LLC. All rights reserved,
including the right of reproduction in whole or in part in any form. SIMON SPOTLIGHT,
READY-TO-READ, and colophon are registered trademarks of Simon & Schuster, Inc.

LIBRARY OF CONGRESS CATALOGING-IN-PUBLICATION DATA

This title was previously cataloged with the following information:

Scieszka, Jon.
 Uh-oh Max / written by Jon Scieszka ; characters and environments developed by
the Design Garage: David Shannon, Loren Long, David Gordon.—1st Aladdin Paperbacks ed.
  p. cm—(Jon Scieszka's Trucktown. Ready-to-roll.)
Summary: When Max gets in trouble after speeding up a ramp, all of his
Trucktown friends try to help out.
ISBN-13: 978-1-4169-4141-5   ISBN-10: 1-4169-4141-X (pbk)
ISBN-13: 978-1-4169-4152-1   ISBN-10: 1-4169-4152-5 (library)
[1. Traffic accidents—Fiction. 2. Trucks—Fiction.] I. Design Garage. II. Title.
PZ7.S41267Uh 2009
[E]—dc22
                    2007027809

978-1-61479-399-1 (reinforced library bound edition)

Spotlight
A Division of ABDO
abdopublishing.com

Max jumps.

Max flies.

"TO THE MAX!"

he cheers.

Max is stuck.
"Call Jack!" Max shouts.

Jack pushes.
No luck. Max is stuck.

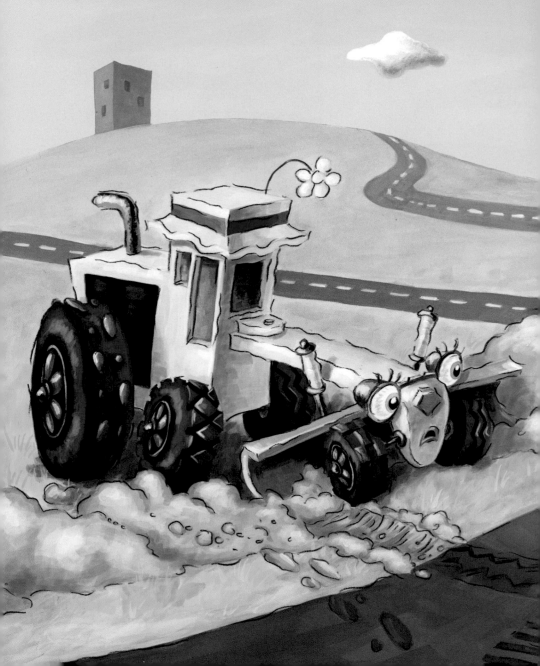

Kat digs.

No luck. Max is stuck.

"Call Gabby!"

Max shouts.

Gabby talks . . .

and talks . . .

and talks.

Really no luck.
Max is **really** stuck.
Who can help?

"Do you want an ice cream?
Do you want an ice cream?
Do you want an ice cream?"

An ice cream won't help.

The Fire Truck twins?

Nope.

Tow Truck Ted?
Of course!

"Hurray for Ted!"

Max zooms.

Max jumps.

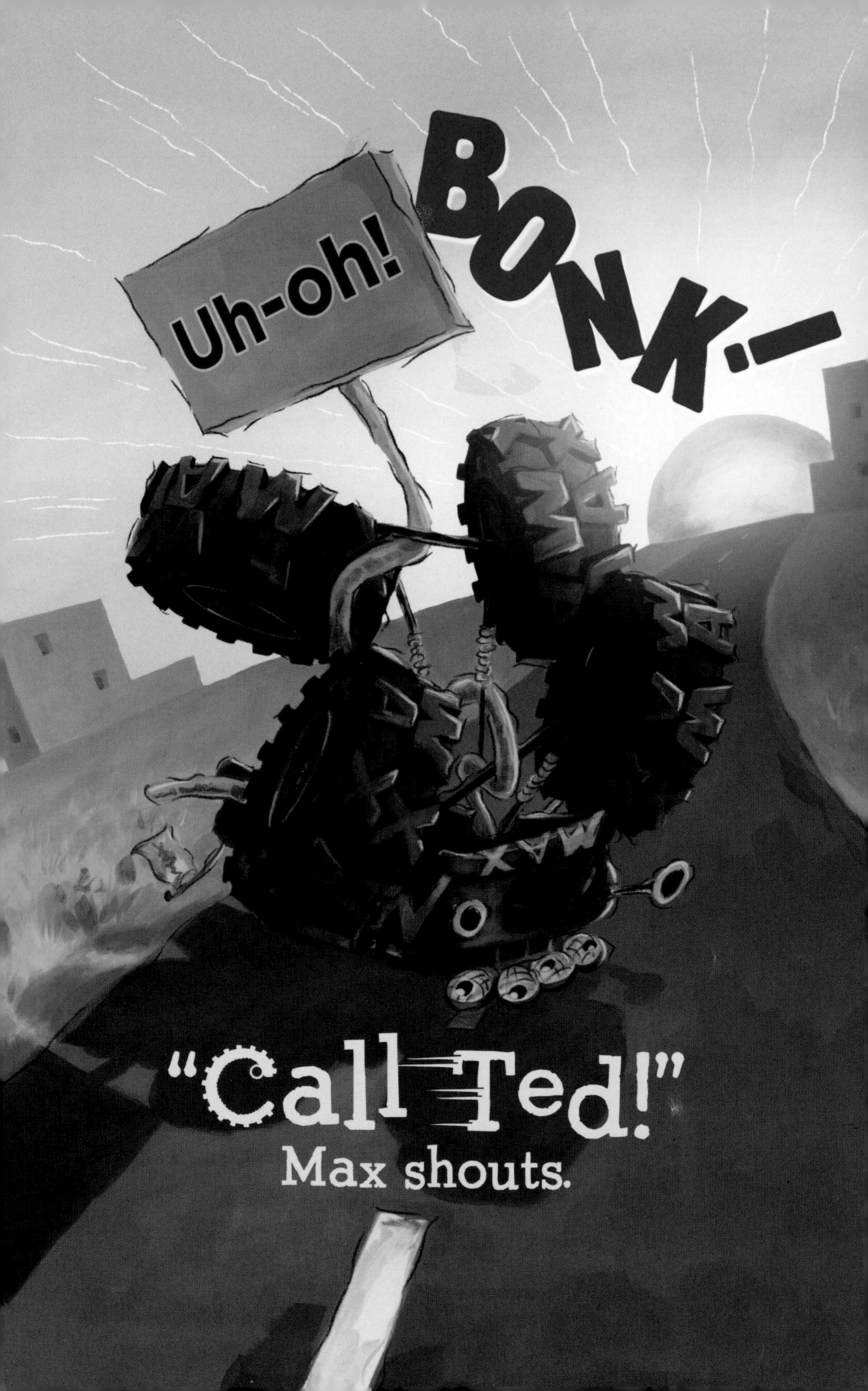

"Call Ted!"
Max shouts.